Identity Thieves

(c) Matthew Russell Lee, Nov 2021

I.

"It's just another Nigerian internet scam case."

That was the message from the Federal Defenders, asking Michael Randall Long to represent one of the minor co-defendants since he had got back on the Criminal Justice Act panel by shooting white fish in the barrel of the insurrection cases in DC.

Long remembered a few of these cases, including one where the defendant cut off his location monitoring bracelet and disappeared.. A dumpy guy from Lagos and then Newark, taking off old ladies with dreams of romance for every cent in their saving account, and then whatever they could borrow.

He'd had the bad luck of getting a judge who was not only a former prosecutor but, it seemed, a victim of love. She went above the guidelines and rather than just appealing Long's client had charged him with ineffective assistance. It was one of the cases cited when the took him off the CJA panel.

But he was back! Maybe on the Gold Coast of Long Island there were no second acts. But here in Foley Square, the old Five Points, redemption was an everyday thing. Long said sure, he'd represent Prince Mohammed Bande, the money laundering car repair maven of East Tremont in

1

The Bronx. It paid just as well as crack dealers and was probably less dangerous.

The takedown had been in the morning, the old 6 am FBI special. By the time Long met Bande in the holding cell outside the SDNY Mag court, it was clear Bande thought everyone was his enemy.

"F*ck you, bro," Bande told him. "I just want you to contact my consulate."

The US had agreement with some countries to always notifying them if one of their nationals was arrested. Long couldn't remember if Nigeria was on the list. But then Bande said more.

"Better you call the UN," he said. "Amina Mohammed, she knows all about this."

Long knew a guy who would be all over this, but he was out of pocket. "Let's just get through the arraignment," he told his shotgun client. "Lemme go out there and see if they're agreeing to bail packages."

Out in the Magistrates Court Judge Vratil had not returned to the bench. A hard-ass AUSA from NYU, Emma Kudlow, was at the prosecutors' table flipping through the file.

"No safety valve," Kudlow told Long curtly, referring the Trump's and Kanye's criminal justice reform law. "We're asking for detention."

"On what grounds?" Long asked.

"Danger and risk of flight," Kudlow told him. "Your guy ran out onto the fire escape when they showed up to arrest him. He's been back and forth to Nigeria three times this year already."

"He has family there," Long said, not knowing if that was true.

"Whatever," Kudlow said, turning her back on him. "Let's see what Judge Vratil says."

Long thought, this case might be a dog.

II.

"All rise!"

Judge Vraitel came in from the side door, gesturing even before she got to the bench that everyone should sit down, don't mind me.

"In the matter of US versus Bande, criminal cause for presentment, will counsel please identify themselves?"

Vratel's clerk Sally Bixby turned on the recording, from behind her enormous computer monitor. Bande was clutching himself and shivering. As always, it was ice cold in the Mag Court.

The case, an identity theft and money laundering conspiracy, was too big to have all of the defendants presented at the same time. Some CJA counsel hung around to watch other lawyers' clients get presented and get or not get released on bond. For Long, time was money. So other than what the Federal Defender William Kandinsky had told him, he was flying blind.

"Michael Randall Long, member of the CJA panel, for Mr. Bande," he said when it was his turn.

"Good afternoon, Mr. Long," Judge Vratil said. "Or good evening." It was already getting dark over the playground visible from the Mag Court's north-looking windows. How many defendants had taken in that view before disappearing into the Bureau of Prisons' ether for years or decades?

Judge Vratil asked, "Mister Bande, do you need the services of an interpreter? Some of your --"

"I speak English," Bande cut in, rarely a good move. "I have a green card. I am a lawful resident."

"Fine," Judge Vratil smirked. "Mr. Long, I'm going to direct the next set of questions to you, and I hope it will be you, in turn, who answers them."

"Yes Judge," Long said. He didn't like to say Your Honor.

"I have before me an affidavit listing Mr. Bande's income and assets. Did you help him fill it out?" Judge Vratil asked.

"I did."

"Give me a moment to review it."

Not all judges took the time. It was never clear to Long what the threshold was. Down in DC, where he had revived his career representing the insurrectionists or breachers, they said the cut off $75,000. But here, it was up to the judge.

"He seems to be selling a lot of cars," Judge Vratil remarked, not looking up from the form.

"I'm just a pass-through," Bande said. "I fix them for people in Nigeria."

Now Judge Vratil looked up. "Mister Long," she said. "I do not want to get into the substance of what may or may not be a defense. I am only trying to establish Mr. Bande's eligibility for appointed counsel." She paused. "I do so find, pending any supplemental information if conditions change or become known to you subsequently, Mr. Long. Do you understand?"

"Yes Judge." Long said that a lot.

"Are we on for an arraignment?" Judge Vratil asked Kudlow.

"No Your Honor," Kudlow answer. "For now only for the detention hearing."

Long wondered if that meant the Kudlow's office would be trying to make Bande into a cooperator. Long didn't much like representing snitches but you had to do what your client wanted. He was sometimes summoned to this room to take on as clients unindicted co-conspirators, to represent them as witnesses and school them on their Fifth Amendment rights and use-immunity. But straight turncoats were not Long's cup of tea.

"Mister Long, I see you standing there, do you have something to say?"

"No Judge. Except, if Mister Bande is not going to be arraigned on the charges, we'd ask for the preliminary hearing in 21 days."

"Or fourteen if I detain him," Vratil remarked. "Let's get to that. What are the government's intentions, Ms. Kudlow?"

"The government seeks to detain Mr. Bande," Kudlow answered.

"On what grounds?" Judge Vratil asked.

"Danger to the community, given the violent acts ascribed to other members of the charged conspiracy," Kudlow said. "But on Mr. Bande, particularly as a risk of flight."

"Is this a presumption case?" Judge Vratil asked.

Even Long knew that it wasn't. That was guns and drugs. This was just money, except for the guns that others listed on the indictment were charged with. Which of course meant that DOJ could try to hang that on Bande.

"We believe that it is," Kudlow said. "But on any standard of the Bail Reform Act, we believe there are no set of conditions that could reasonably assure Mister Bande's return to court."

Bande blurted out, "I'll come back, Your Excellency. I need to run my business--"

"*Mist*er Long," Judge Vratil said. "Please tell your client he has not only the right, but for now the duty, to remain silent."

"Yes Judge," Long said. He leaned over to Bande, taking down his cloth mask and whispered "You need to stop talking. I'm trying to get you released on bond."

"Fine job you're doing too, man," Bande said, loud enough that not only the two Marshals sitting behind him but even the audio recording must have heard him. Thank God it was almost never that anyone ordered these presentment proceedings transcribed.

Almost.

"So tell me about it, Ms. Kudlow," Judge Vratil said. "It being the government's burden."

"Thank you your Honor. When law enforcement went to arrest Mr. Bande this morning on the warrant you signed last night, at first he pretended that he was not there. Then he was found running out the back fire escape without his shoes on." Kudlow paused and smiled broadly, too broadly for Long's taste. "He is the very definition of a flight risk."

"I don't have my dictionary with me," Judge Vratil deadpanned. "But if the facts as the Government alleges them are true, it does seem to be according to Websters, or to Hoyle's, which ever."

Bande pulled at Long's sleave. "What she means," he said.

"Can I have a moment with my client?" Long asked.

"Certainly, Mister Long. Marshals, can you take these two gentlemen back into the holding cell to confer?"

"Yes Your Honor," the burly one said. Long has spoken to him a few times. But only about weather. Or then COVID. Now, about the limited selection in the partially re-opened Cafeteria on the eighth floor. Long didn't know his name.

Burly gestured to Bande to stand up, not easy as he feet were shackled. "You know the drill, counselor," he told Long. Yes, Long did. He didn't much like being in the holding cell. It often made him wonder, sometimes suddenly, what it would be like to never be able to walk out. Put him in his client's lace-less shoes, so to speak.

III.

It was even colder in the holding cell than it was out in the Mag court. And Long could barely concentrate on what Bande was telling him, given the guy with the face tattoos who was glaring at him. Had Long represented him and failed? He couldn't remember. But he got enough to make his argument. Vratil probably already knew what she was going to do, Long thought. Everyone was just playing their role, building their record.

"We're ready," Long told Burly, who nodded.

"You saw what they tried to pass off as pizza this week?" Burly asked.

Long had. That day he'd instead gotten the four dollar - $4.12 with tax -- tomato and onion salad in a plastic box, so cold it hurt his teeth then made his breath stink the rest of the afternoon and probably longer. "Yeah," he said. "Oklahoma style pizza." He made that up. He could do that sometimes.

Burly laughed. "This place," he said.

Back out in the Mag Court, Judge Vratil had left the bench.

"Are you prepared to proceed, Mr. Long?" Sally Bixby asked him.

"As prepared as I'll ever be," Long answered. Then added, "As we'll ever be." Any loss had to be shared.

Vratil pre-ordered those present to sit down, or not stand up in the first place. "OK Mr. Long," she began. "Tell me why your client ran out the fire escape. This, I've got to hear."

"It's his upbringing," Long said. He hoped he wasn't showing any smile. "In Nigeria, anyone can bang on your door and claim to be law enforcement. They could just be there to rob you, or worse. So Mister Bande, and I'm not saying it was reasonable, or that you or I would do it, he went out the window until he could find out more."

It was Vratil who smiled. "I'll have to check Human Rights Watch's report on Nigeria, maybe make it part of the record," she said.

Long knew HRW, at least its bosses in New York, to have their own human rights problems. But whatever it took. "I can send your chambers the Amnesty International report," he said, gesturing at his smart phone, blinking on the table. The cell service in the Mag court was terrible. Thankfully Judge Vratil didn't taken him up on it.

"While it's a novel argument," she said, "it's a bit too novel, at least for me, at least for today. I'm going to deny the motion for release on bond, without prejudice. If you get more, Mr Long, or can come up with a bail package that could address this run-down-the-fire-escape issue, just contact Ms. Bixby and we'll have you come in. You might want to waive your client's presence in advance. Because he'll be going to the MDC for the foreseeable future."

"This is unfair!" Bande shouted out. "They pay me to fix up cars and ship them to Nigeria, that's all!"

"Then that will be your defense," Judge Vratil cut him off. "Mr. Long, you have to do better."

"I'll try, Judge," Long said.

And he would.

IV.

Slumped in the back row of the Mag Court, tweeting on his dying smart phone plugged into the outlet on the side, Kurt Wheelock took notice when Nigeria was mentioned. Before he'd been thrown out of the UN he had started writing, if blogging could be called that, about the conflicts in Biafra and in River State, the arrests and extraditions of Nnamdi Kanu and Igboho, and the UN's telling silence.

But what did any of that have to do with a gang of car thieves in The Bronx?

Wheelock would come to the Magistrates Court at the end of each reporting day, after running between listening to cases on three phone lines in the otherwise empty Press Room in 40 Foley and the in-person trials and evidentiary hearings held in the big courtrooms on the top three floors of 500 Pearl Street.

The latter would run to five - they'd stay later only if a jury was deliberating - then Kurt would take the elevator down to Eight, where the cafeteria was, then the other elevator bank down to Five, where the Mag Court was next to the in-court office of the SDNY prosecutors.

Several times he'd been ordered out of the fifth floor hallway, or made to face the wall and not look as a confidential or anonymous witness walked in or out of the prosecutors' office. Rather than continue openly complaining about it, he'd taken to mentioning it on podcasts and vlogs, where what he said wasn't subject to word-search. But still it was found, by some he wished would look away. So it went with social media.

Kurt knew both lawyers on this Nigeria case, the third of six proceeding he was to witness that early evening. But he hadn't caught the docket number when the defendant was first brought it, and had mis-written his name as Banty in his reporters notebook.

Kurt had thumbed slow, cryptic tweets about the case before - a truck driver from California caught unloading fentanyl along with lettuce in the Bronx' Hunts Point market - and would the one after, a dentist at St. Barnabas accused of sexual molesting his anesthetized patients. But it was hard to even tweet about a case, if you had neither the defendant's name nor docket number.

But Banty running out the fire escape to escape the police, who might have been fake police Kurt heard Mike Long argue without success, was the kind of detail he liked to put on his courthouse blog. So when the case was over, he left his phone plugged in and asked Sally Bixby when she walked the paperwork to the room next door where bonds were signed, "Do you have the docket number of that last case, US versus Banty?"

Bixby looked at him, and down at the sheaf of papers she was holding. "It's Bande," she said. "B-A-N-D-E. And it doesn't have a docket number yet."

Even Kurt knew that was unlikely. Cases like this began with an MJ number, for "Magistrate," then graduated up to CR when a District Judge was assigned. But he did his best not to fight with the law clerks or staff in the room next door, much less the Court Security Officers and Marshals, after what had happened to him at the UN.

"That's great, I can go from there," Kurt said.

But could he? Would he?

V.

Back in his office over the Ali Baba fruit stand Michael Randall Long had a court appearance to make - by Zoom, as it happened. It was a Capitol breach defendant whom the Federal Public Defenders in DC had sent his way, or doled out to him.

Rather than a crossbow hunter from Texas or old man from Alabama with moonshine jar Molotov cocktails from which all gas had evaporated through the jar-holes incompletely sealed by golf tees, this was a doozy.

Oswaldo Steiner, before fighting with Capitol Police, had worked at the U.S. State Department.

Long hadn't had much of a chance to confer with Steiner: he was in the DC Jail, in the J6 unit. But all Long had to do today was plead not guilty to the superseding indictment.

New video of Steiner bragging about his connections to the last Administration while waggling a police baton like a baseball bat had emerged. Judge Reggie Walton would probably grant the government's motion to set another status sixty days out, and exclude Speedy Trial Act time until then. But you never knew.

You also never knew who else was on the phone. There was a public call-in line, listening only, the usage of which was not monitored. At least as far as Long knew. Lawyers on such hybrid calls, and judges too it seems, could forget about the public listen-in or voyeur line as they called it.

Long often wrote down on a Post-it (TM) note on his desk looking out at Chatham Square and the SDNY court: "Remember the Public." It meant, Remember the Public Line.

"Good to see you, Mister Long," Judge Walton said. Long had enough of these cases that he got this greeting sometime. Or maybe Walton was just reading from the docket, the notice of appearance that the Federal Public Defenders had put in for him when they'd dumped the case on him.

"Glad to be here, Judge," Long said. He hoped the police sirens outside, prisoners being brought into state court at 100 Centre mostly likely, wasn't so loud Walton would comment on it. Though it did set a certain mood.

"So this is a second arraignment on a superseder, I take it?" Walton asked.

Long was trying to take himself off mute when the AUSA, one of the insufferable pontificators about democracy and the shame the insurrection had brought on the country, answered instead. "Yes, Your Honor. It seems Mr. Steiner was bragging that day about his State Department work."

"I see," Walton said. "So you've added charges."

"Yes Your Honor. It's particularly galling when a person uses his or her connection to the government to try to overthrow the government."

Long couldn't let this one slide. "We're pleading not guilty, by the way," he said. "And we don't concede that the exercise of First Amendment rights is the same as trying to overthrow the government."

"That ship has sailed," Judge Walton said. "But I'm sure I'll hear your arguments, going forward in this case."

"Indeed you will," Long said, trying to be equally insufferable.

"You've pled your client not guilty," Walton went on. "I'll set a status sixty days out" - that phrasing again - "and exclude time. Does the government have a motion?"

"Yes your Honor," the AUSA said. "This is one of the largest prosecutions in US history, with terabyte upon terabyte of video evidence to review and produce to the defendants. We have a duty under Brady to provide Mr. Long with all possibly exculpatory evidence --" The AUSA paused then snarked, "Not that we've found any, or are likely to."

"Just give us the video," Long said. "Since I know Speedy Trial Act time will be excluded even if we oppose it."

"You're right, Mr. Long," Judge Walton said. "It's by operation of law at this point, Chief Judge's standing order."

Then why do you ask for a motion from the government, Long thought. "Yes judge," he said.

"See you in sixty days," Judge Walton said. "We are adjourned. Watch out for the virus."

The virus was the least of Long's problems. At least so he thought.

VI.

Kurt Wheelock might have mis-heard Bande as Banty, and not gotten his case's docket number - but he had heard and written down the address in The Bronx from which Banty had run out the fire escape and made or shown himself to be a risk of flight. So Kurt went up there to check it out.

Bande's World of Luxury Rides was on Park Avenue, not the Park Avenue with flower beds in the median strip and park benches named after old couples searching for eternity but the hard-scrapple Park Avenue of the Bronx.

The Metro North train whizzed by down in the railroad cut and there were on the block at least two burned out cars with no tires on them, not luxury at all, perhaps never luxury.

Bande's location, on the other hand, had the ubiquitous Mercedes peace sign painted on its bright yellow tin sign and a green and white flag Kurt recognized as that of Nigeria. The big roll-down gate cars or even trucks pulling cars could drive in and out of was shut, but a door in it was open.

Kurt looked in.

"What do you want?" a voice asked from the darkness inside, not exactly friendly. It came from over in a corner amid a shower of yellow sparks. Welding.

"I wanted to meet Mr. Bande," he answered. Not possible, but not exactly a lie.

"You a cop?"

Kurt laughed. "Nah," he said. FTP.

"He's, uh, not here."

Kurt decided as he often did, probably too often, to try to move things forward. "I heard he got arrested."

"Then why you come here looking for him?"

Fair question. "I thought he got out on bail."

The speaker emerged, welding mask still on, the torch dribbling sparks. Menacing, Kurt took it as. But he was the one who had interrupted.

"No man, they kept him locked up, at the MDC in Brooklyn." The guy paused then said, it seemed hopefully, "You looking for a car? These are already committed to Nigeria. But we got others coming in, big crash on the Cross Bronx, I could get you something nice off the books."

Kurt's days of owning cars were gone. But this could be a way to find out more. "The right price, for sure," he said. He wrote down the number to his cell phone, which was also his printing press, his podcasting studio and camera for vlogs. A veritable Gutenberg, with no control over the platforms his content went out on. Little control of anything else either. But there was something about this case.

VII.

"We got an offer."

The Federal Defenders, who represented the lead named defendant in Bande's case, were calling a meeting of the other counsel in the case. Legally, each defendant had their own interest which their assigned CJA lawyer was supposed to advance.

But since the Federal Defenders were in charge of which lawyers got on the CJA panel, when they said "jump" the CJAs like Michael Randall Long replied, "How high?"

Even though the Defenders had their office just across Foley Square on Duane Street, the meeting was by Zoom. Long fired up his ASUS, choosing the Thurgood Marshall staircase as his backdrop, and signed in. Typing in his whole name, all that the others saw was "Michael Randall."

"The US Attorney wants to plead this case out," Federal Defender William Kandinsky told them. "It seems like they're under some pressure, I can't entirely figure it out, but it if helps our clients so be it."

Long nodded, but thought: I don't need lessons in legal ethics from this pencil-neck.

"Anyway it's kind of a package deal. A year and a day for each defendant, in a camp, no supervised release," Kandinsky continued.

No question it was a good deal, Long thought. Or an attractive offer. But why were they offering this? Was there a better plea agreement to be had?

"The offer has an expiration date and they said it's key that all of the defendants get on board," Kandinsky said. "Though the second part, they'll never put in writing."

Of course not, Long thought. He asked, "Did they rough anyone up during the take down?"

"Not that I know of," Kandinsky answered.

"Wire tap without a warrant?"

"I saw the warrant," Kandinsky said. "It looks fine. Unless they back-dated it."

Long wondered why Federal Defender Kandinsky had already gotten discovery like the warrant, and he hadn't. This, he didn't just think to himself. He asked.

"Kudlow told me they reached out with the discovery to each of us but you didn't respond," Kandinsky told Long with a smirk. "Maybe it's in your spam folder."

Long nodded, and checked. There was nothing from Kudlow there.

"I'm going to have to think about the offer," he finally said, unlike the others who'd already given a provisional Yes.

"To check with your client, right?" Kandinsky asked, or said.

"Need to think about it," Long said. He gave the obligatory wave, the sarcasm of which may have been lost on Kandinsky, and hit "Leave Meeting" at the bottom of the screen.

VIII.

Sunset Park, Brooklyn was New York City's third Chinatown, after Flushing and the Mott Street original. A little more raw, a little more authentic. Michael Randall Long stopped in for a plate of steaming and peppered mustard greens before heading to the MDC. He hated having to come out here to visit his clients. But this offer required an in-person visit, or it could be ineffective assistance of counsel.

"No way, bro," Bande told him, when they finally got settled, still within earshot of the Corrections Officers.

"The Federal Defender's telling me that all your co-defendants are going to take the offer," Long said. "I'm not telling you what to do. I just wonder why you think they're taking it."

"First off, they all U.S. citizens, one way or another. They serve their one year or whatever --"

"Year and a day is less than a year," Long introjected, always glad to explain that. "It makes you eligible for what they call Good Time. So really it's like ten months."

"That ain't the problem," Bande continued. "They citizens so after their time is done, they're out and back at it. Me, they gonna deport."

It was true. A green card was no defense to this. You plead to a felony, you get removed.

"I could try to talk to them," Long said wanly. It was operation of law. A felony plea would mean removal. Unless....

"Do you think you might wanna cooperate," Long asked.

Bande glared at him. "You crazy, man? These people don't play. They fuckin' kill you" -- he snapped his fingers, and a guard looked over -- "like that." Bande paused then said loudly to the guard, "What you looking at?"

"Tell you client to keep it down," the guard told Long.

"Understood," Long said.

Bande leaned closer and whispered. "It's like I told you - reach out to Amina Mohammed at the UN. She know all about this, she know all of us."

"But why?" Long said, wondering why a United Nations official would know a guy fixing cars in the South Bronx, and a bunch of email hacker and romance scammers. Maybe it was that.

"Just do what I say," Bande told Long. "Tell her I'm in lock up and I'm worry, she got to help me."

"I don't want to get you killed," Long said. The ultimate ineffective assistance of counsel.

"Let me worry about that," Bande said. "Just tell her."

But how? Long figured the UN must take a call from a lawyer, especially one that might be complaining about maltreatment in the U.S. prison system. Right?

"Okay," Long said. "I'll give it a go."

Long has always wanted to work in human rights.

IX.

Paulo de Souza was the UN's lawyer and it was a matter of pride to him how little work he did. It reflected how little the UN had to do - not that the UN didn't create many of the tort, even mass or toxic tort, situation that drove law school classes. But the UN didn't have to answer for them. And the symbol of this was de Souza drinking coffee with his factotum in the UN Bar over the East River.

He or they were there, flush with impunity, when the email from Michael Randall Long came through. I am a lawyer, the message began, and de Souza almost immediately hit Delete. Others might have to continue reading threats. He and the UN didn't.

But the message mentioned prison, and it mention de Souza's number two boss, Amina J. Mohammed. De Souza thought Amina, as he called her, was an empty power tunic. But she had the ear of his real boss, Antonio Guterres, his fellow Portuguese, and so defending her might raise de Souza even higher in his countryman's short eyes.

"Set up a meeting with this guy," de Souza said, laying his phone down face up on the table cloth he has already stained with the spoon used to stir his cappuccino. "And call Benami. It's time that fancy Moroccan did some work for a change."

X.

Raad Benami was on the toilet when he got the message from de Souza, albeit second hand. He spent more and more of his time seeking to void himself of bile. But his hatred of Number Two animated him.

Sure he resented Guterres and his arrogance as Guterres protected his European cronies like Fabrizio Hochschild while leaving UN officials of color - that's how

Benami referred to himself, on one of his anonymous Twitter accounts - out in the cold, fighting for the scraps.

But Benami found Amina J. Mohammed the UN's Number Two even more insufferable, moving around with a huge entourage and accomplishing nothing, except making her mentor and boss, the military dictator Buhari, bullet proof in UN world.

The very week that Amina J. Mohammed - you had to use the J as there was another Amina Mohamed, a foreign minister of Kenya who actually got some things done - was supposed to show up and take her no-show job, the feminist or at least feminine sidekick of the short fat man Guterres who like Harvey Weinstein stole everything from women, she stayed in Abuja and back-dated six thousand CITES certificates to send endangered rosewood from Nigeria and Cameroon to China.

Benami still knew the blogger who, when he asked Amina J. Mohammed or really her and Guterres' spokesman Stephane Dujarric, got himself first caged with UN security in the diplomatic hallway he used to run free, then thrown out altogether.

It was a shame, because until then Benami had often used the blogger to leak anti UN material to try to move up, Machiavellian, through the ranks. Benami still leaked to him sometimes, but it was harder to have an impact on the UN when you get banned from entering.

So de Souza wanted Benami to attend his meeting with a lawyer threatening to sue Amina. Sure, Benami could do that. If he could only get off and stay off the toilet long enough.

XI.

It was time for Michael Long to speak with Oswaldo Steiner, down in the DC Jail. When Long went to DC he liked to take Amtrak, the Sleepy Joe express. With a mask on the whole way, he didn't breathe as easy. But the abandoned factories along the sides of the railroad tracks still made his heart race.

Steiner was effusive, as if he had verbal diarrhea: a diplomat, as well perhaps as an insurrectionist or domestic terrorist. Spoiled rich kid, really, Long thought. But he was here to listen.

"The stuff I said about Trump, I see they're gonna hold it against me," Steiner said. "Isn't that against the First Amendment?"

"Normally, maybe," Long answered. "But once you commit a physical act in the real world that they can punish you for, like going into Congress without permission, the other stuff comes in."

"When I went in the police weren't even trying to stop us," Steiner said.

"Did you think it was legal?" Long asked. Then, getting no answer, he added, "Don't answer that." Let the judge ask, Long thought. It was Steiner's funeral, or jail time. It was time to change the topic and Long had something to ask.

"What do you know about Nigeria? And maybe relatedly, about this lady who's the UN Deputy Secretary General, Amina Mohammed?"

Steiner's face changed; he even emitted a short laugh or snort. "You mean Amina JAY Mohammed?" Steiner said. "She's corrupt as hell. She's the one who should be in this jail."

"What do you mean?"

"On the Africa Desk at State they used to say, Behind the dead bodies of Biafra, and elsewhere in Nigeria, is that smiling Fulani fraud at the UN, blabbing about the SDGs."

Long, now taking notes, heard STDs. He's ask later, or Google. Because Steiner was plowing on.

"She ran interference not only for Buhari's killings, which he probably could have covered up himself using all the oil money the country was cursed with - she also got involved in Cameroon, which keep saying it has oil off the coast of the Anglophone zones without really producing. So Paul Biya, the forty year dictator there, needs more outside help than Buhari. And he gets it from Paris, and from the UN."

Long's interest was more practical. "Why do you think Amina J. Mohammed might be involved in a gang of car thieves, or really, identity theft and money launderers, operating in the US?"

"Damn," Steiner said. "You get this from another client?"

"I can't say," Long answered. Attorney - client privilege was usually about not telling the government, or another co-defendant in the same case. Maybe he hadn't thought this through enough.

"Cause I could use that to get out of here," Steiner said. "Or at least reduce my sentence."

Long didn't say anything. In for a penny, in for a pound. "Humor me for now," he said. "Why would she do it? If it were true."

Steiner looked full of himself as he produced his theory.

"Beyond personal corruption, of which like Guterres there is a lot, Buhari in Nigeria needs a stream of money to fight his war against Biafra, just like Biya needs in to kill the Anglophones who, I bet, wish they'd joined Nigeria and not Cameroon when the UN screwed them."

Steiner paused and said, "Sorry counselor," apparently about the F-bomb. Long didn't care.

"Anyway there's a theory that some of the Nigerian scams, the hacking and the phishing and the sale of unrelated goods to make the money clean, is to create a flow of blood money to Buhari and Biya that doesn't have to be reported to the IMF."

"What?" Long asked. This acronym might be more important than the STDs.

"International Monetary Fund," Steiner said, looking pleased with himself. "Both governments need those IMF loans to prop themselves up. If you can fund your internal war with a separate stream of funds it all goes easier."

"And this is well known?" Long demanded.

"It's a theory," Steiner said. "But yeah. I think it's true."

Like with the STDs, it was something Long would have to Google. "I'm going to tell the judge we want a trial date," he told Steiner as he stood up.

"You have a duty to use everything you have to help me, right?" Steiner asked, or said.

Or pull out of the case for a conflict of interest, Long thought. "I fight for you," he said.

* * *

On the train ride back, with an avocado and iceberg lettuce salad they called the Californian at the Chop't re-opened in Union Station, Long used Amtrak Wi-Fi to read about Biafra and a place he'd never heard of, Ambazonia.

Even widening his search he found only one website, one he knew that made this allegation, though clumsily, half-informed. Long would go to the meeting with de Souza, try to put some pressure on this Amina J. Mohammed for his client Bande, and take it from there.

XII.

The meeting took place in the UN, on the 38th floor, on Deputy Amina J. Mohammed's side of it, not Guterres scam cave to the north. Michael Randall Long has insisted

28

on it, telling de Souza that since it had to do with the Deputy Secretary General - that's how she demanded people refer to her - he wanted to be sure that she heard what he had to say.

"But she won't be the one answering any questions," de Souza respond. He thought, maybe it would be good for them on the 38th floor to see that he did for them, and that he didn't just hang around all day with his factotum, on the UN bar and elsewhere.

"Of course," Long said. "I never question another lawyer's client unless it's cross examination time." It wasn't really true, but Long liked the sound of it.

From this office above Ali Baba, Long went west along the always under construction Worth Street to historic Foley Square. He went into the subway entrance on the Square and waited for the express 4 train at the front of the platform.

Usually these days he would start on the other side, Brooklyn bound to Cadman Plaza and the EDNY court there. The 4-5-6 IRT line was just as unreliable in both directions.

From Foley Square, the 4 train inched past graffitied subway walls then gathered speed, flashing past the last Chinatown stop at Canal, Spring and Bleeker, past the closed down K-Mart in the Astor Place station and stopped at Union Square.

More people got on, and Long decided to give his seat to an enormously obese woman. If she stood in front of him he might miss getting off at Grand Central - 42nd Street.

She thanked him and Long felt appropriately faux humanitarian for a trip to the UN. He saw the blue glass town down 43rd Street, where homeless men ate sandwiches on large rocks meant to calm traffic. He passed Tudor Village and went down the Isaiah staircase, something about beat swords into plowshares. "And then selling them at the price of gold," Long said to himself, happy with the turn of phrase.

He turned north on First Avenue; he was not allowed to enter the 42nd Street staff entrance or the 45th Street diplomats' greet point. There was a tourist entrance on 46th Street and Long got on line.

The other tourists had paid money to come visit this mausoleum; they showed their tickets to UN Security. "What's your business here?" a tall guard, Long made him for ex-NYPD, demanded.

"I have an appointment," Long said. "With Amina J. Mohammed."

The guard looked skeptical. "The Deputy Secretary General? Show me."

Long took out his cell phone, wondering about the UN's right to search and seizure. It might be absolute, here on their international territory. No Fourth Amendment, and from what he heard no First Amendment either.

"Lemme call upstairs," the guard said. "If it checks out I'll be waiting for you on the other side of the metal checks."

Long nodded, thinking, don't they also make ghost guns out of plastic now?

When it was his turn he took off his belt like in an airport and put his files in the gray plastic bin. Still the alarm when off when he walked through. "Try your shoes," an Eastern European sounding guard told him. He did, but still the buzzer rang.

"It's OK," a voice boomed from the other side of the magnetometer. "He's got an appointment." It was the ex NYPD. He said to Long, "I'll take you up."

The Secretaries General had their own elevator, on the other side of the UN General Assembly's checkerboard floor. It zipped straight up to 38, where four more guards were waiting, to make sure Long didn't turn to the left when he got off. That was Big Tony's lair.

"Hello Mr. Long, I am Kola Aluko, the Deputy's chief of staff," a tall man told him. "Come. She and the Under Secretary General are waiting for you."

That would be de Souza. He and a guy Long had not idea who he was met them in the hall. "Remember, no questions to the DSG," de Souza hissed. "This is Raad Benami, one of our senior advisers."

Long handed the guy his card. You never knew. Soon they were in a room looking not back at Grand Central but east over the River, and Queens and Long Island.

"Breathtaking, isn't it," a woman in a tunic with a white heard scarf said. "I am Amina J. Mohammed, the Deputy Secretary General of the United Nations. I hear that one of my fellow Nigerians has been talking about me."

Long looked over at de Souza. He'd said he wouldn't question this lady, but if she questioned him... Long took the opportunity.

"Yes, a man who is detained and charged with identity theft and money laundering."

Amina J. Mohammed cut in: "How they vilify us Nigerians. What is his name?"

"Mohammed Bande," Long said. Amina didn't bat an eyelid.

"And what is he saying?"

Long decided to go for it. "That you knew about the scheme, of accepting wires from defrauded American businesses and laundering the money as repaired luxury cars shipped to Nigeria. And that the real purpose was to raise money for when he called a righteous war to maintaining territorial integrity, on both Biafra and some part of Cameroon."

De Souza jumped up at the second part of this. "Mr. Long, I'm going to have to--"

"It's okay," Amina said. "I'd rather know what Mr. Bande is saying." She looked back at Long. "You know it's all lies, don't you?"

Long raised the stakes. "I have a client who works, or worked, in the US State Department. He tells me this is an open secret down there."

One they never talk about, Amina thought. "Oh really? Who?" she asked.

Long shook his head. "Attorney client."

"Exactly the phrase I was going to us," de Souza said. "I think this meeting is over."

Long looked at Amina, expecting her to call off her Brazilian dog or terrier. But she just sat there, and Kola Aluko nodded at de Souza. He seemed to push a button under the table and suddenly ex-NYPD came in.

"Let me show you out," the tall cop said. Then in the hall, "That didn't last long."

"That my name, Long." On the ground floor he was marched around the traffic circle with its fountain known for spreading Legionnaires Disease, and though a gate next to where the diplomats' cars drove in. "Hope you enjoyed your visit to the United Nations. Don't... come again."

XIII.

Raad Benami hadn't said a word in the meeting; even outside Amina J. Mohammed's conference room he had only nodded, when the ambulance chaser Long handed him his business card.

But afterward, Benami had a lot to say, not to the attendees but someone he knew would be driver crazier by what Long had blurted, and would maybe help Benami in the process.

Benami would have lunched at Il Postino and expensed it to the UN, but he might be spotted there. He told the blogger to meet him at their regular, the Korean deli on 47th Street with the tables to eat at in the back.

Benami got there ten minutes early so he could empty his bowels, or try to, before Kurt arrived. Even so, he came out five minutes later and Kurt was already at a table, watching some Premier League football match.

Try the bibimbap, Benami said by rote. I've already ordered mine.

"I'll use their salad bar," Kurt said. It would be fast and cheaper and he was eager to hear what Benami had summoned him here for.

Kurt got three artificial eel sushi rolls and a dallop of wasabi, and tortellini under a lumpy cream sauce. Benami looked at the latter longingly and said, as it to himself, I don't think that's good for you.

"I don't have it every day," Kurt said. That honor was reserved for the dubious pork dumplings for $1.25 on Mosco Street by the courthouse, or when he felt flush, the three dollar pork and cabbage version at Tasty Dumpling around the corner on Mulberry Street. He said down and popped a Wasabi-ed eel sushi in his mouth. "I'm all ears," he said.

"I was at a meeting, Benami started, as he usually did with Kurt. "And this lawyer representing a Nigerian who is in Federal lockup for some sort of cars for cash scam yelled at Amina J. Mohammed that she's part of a scheme to raise money for Buhari --"

Kurt coughed and some wasabi flew out of his mouth. "You mean the guy Banty," he corrected himself, "Bande who was arrested for identify theft?"

"I don't know the particulars," Benami said. "But yeah, that's who the lawyer represents. And Bande sent him to talk to de Souza and Amina about the scam. To threaten them, basically."

Kurt loved it. "Was Guterres there?"

"Just down the hall."

"How did it end?" Kurt asked. He could be journalistic sometimes.

"Badly. Long was basically thrown out of the UN."

Kurt thought, Like me. And he recognized the name when Benami flashed him the business card, but wouldn't let him take it. This Michael Randall Long had a long reach. Kurt thought Long might not know what to do with these Nigeria and UN scam info. But Kurt knew. At least what to try.

XIV.

The Metropolitan Detention Center in Brooklyn had come to replace the MCC in lower Manhattan, after Jeffrey Epstein died there. Epstein's girlfriend / procurer Ghislaine Maxwell replaced him as the MDC's highest profile inmate, and even threatened to complain to the United Nations about conditions. (Kurt thought that like Ghislaine was rich, given that the UN had let Ghislaine hold a press conference he had attended, for some fig leaf of an oceans NGO called Terramar, and that Guterres' head of Partnerships Amir Dossal was on the board of directors of Terramar).

But the bad conditions impacted other, lower profile prisoners as well. A former DEA agent who dabbled in child porn had died the very day he was convicted. So the inmates watched their backs, especially when they were extracted from the cells before dawn for transfer to which ever Federal court was processing them, EDNY in Cadman Plaza or SDNY in lower Manhattan.

Mohammed Bande had a status conference with Judge Vratil and so they woke him up at four. There was already clanking and moans and threats from guards as they led him out to the transport. And then, just like that, a figure darted out from a supposedly locked cell and shanked him.

One deep penetration, right through the ribs and into the heart. A spurt of blood leaped out at the guard in front of him, who seemed to be ready for it - was that a plastic tarp? Bande didn't have time to made it out. He was dead before the ambulance, at last, arrived. Judge Vratil would have to wait.

Forever.

XV.

Kurt had seen on PACER that Bande had a status conference before Judge Vratil. There was still a call-in line, unlike for the suddenly disappearing trials of Ghislaine Maxwell, R.Kelly and Theranos' Elizabeth Holmes. But Kurt decided to go in person, to see Bande in the flesh.

Vratil's courtroom deputy Sally Bixby looked up when Kurt came into the courtroom and picked a seat in the next to last row of the gallery, putting his backpack down. Judge and clerk exchanged glances - they were in synch like pitcher and catcher, or like horse and jockey, it just wasn't clear who played which role sometimes - but it was Vratil who was allowed to speak on the record. Other than the call of the case.

"In the matter of the United States versus Bande, it appears that the defendant has not been produced," Bixby called out, seemingly for the court reporter.

Judge Vratil turned it into a question: "Is that correct, Mister Marshal?"

The Marshal, one that Kurt recognized from the fourth floor of 500 Pearl and from the Mag Court, nodded but didn't answer. He stood up, the handcuffs, keys and mace jangling on his belt, and walked over to AUSA Kudlow, spoke to her covering his mouth like a baseball manager to a pitcher on the mound. Unintentional intentional walk?

Kudlow spoke up. "Your Honor, there's been a development in the MDC on which we'll be filing a letter with the court." She paused. "Under seal."

Michael Randall Long had been scrolling through his phone but now stood up. "He's my client, Your Honor," he said. "I think I need to be given a copy of the letter, and be told right now, what the government knows."

Vratil looked into the gallery, where Kurt was not the only one. "Let's do this in my robing room," she said. "We are adjourned."

* * *

The implication was that Kurt should now leave the courtroom, that the proceeding was over. But he took it more like a break in the proceeding, from which Judge Vratil would have to return and put on the record the outcome of the sealed robing room discussion. So he waited. And waited.

Ten minutes into the wait when Kurt checked his phone he had a strange notification or advertisement from Chase Manhattan, which he still called the bank he'd first opened with as Chemical back in The Bronx: "Now that you've bought a car, did you know that we offer bundled insurance in the JPMorgan Chase family?"

A monopolist's family, Kurt thought, what a rich idea. But he had sure not bought any vehicle. So what the hell was going on? His phone was slow, a mixture of low memory and bad cell reception in this courtroom, and to call the 800 number from in here made no sense. So Kurt waited until first Bixby then Kudlow then Long came out from the door behind Judge Vratil's bench.

Bixby looked surprised to see him, for the first time. "All rise!" she said. "The Honorable Elizabeth Vratil!"

Vratil entered and took to the bench, as they called it. "We're back on the record in US versus Bande," she said. "It appears there's been an accident in the MDC. I am ordering the government to file a status letter by this time tomorrow, by email to my chamber with a copy to Mister Long. We are adjourned."

Vratil stood up and so, after a time, did Kurt. Sally Bixby opened the door for Vratil, then followed her out. Kudlow said to Long, I'm sure I'll get you something tomorrow morning early, or even tonight.

"I might file something with the BOP," Long said. He remembered that the Federal Defenders had done that, in the case of the ex-DEA short eyes.

"That would be your prerogative," Kudlow said, as she picked up her binder and headed out of the courtroom. In the back Kurt stood up and walked toward the front. "Not now," Long told him. "There's a few things I need to check first. We can meet in the usual place."

The two men in suits were still in the front row and heard this. "It's about that other case," Kurt said loudly, probably too loudly. By then Long had followed Kudlow out of the courtroom, and gotten into the elevator with her. Kurt as usually took the stairs. But he jogged down them faster than usual.

XVI.

Down in the Press Room Kurt studied his phone with its half shattered screen more closely. Not only was Chase Bank congratulating him on having bought a car -- his balance had been run down past zero. Everything he had saved up was gone. The insanely Pollyanna part of himself whispered, At least now I'd obviously qualify for appointed counsel. But how would he live?

He opened a chat box on the Chase Bank website but the response was pure A.I. - Sure I can help you with that today. Please tell me a little more about your problem. It was just a fancier version of Press 1 for You're Screwed.

There was a Chase Bank branch out in Chatham Square, just past the fruit stand Michael Randall Long's office was over. There was a line, and a security guard. Kurt waited, with his phone open to the screen now showing the negative balance. The guard gestured to him. You Next.

"I didn't spent this," Kurt told the teller. "It wasn't me."

"Did you give password to anyone else?" the clerk asked, looking suspicious. Classic Big Bank: blame the victim.

"Never," Kurt said, and that was true.

"Then how they withdraw it?" the clerk demanded. Staring into a computer screen that Kurt outside the bullet proof glass couldn't see, the clerk said, "It says here you already shipped your car overseas."

"Oh really? Where?"

The clerk smirked. "Nigeria," he said.

The revenge of Bande, Kurt thought. Or maybe of his co-conspirator up at Bande's Luxury Cars. A real Park Avenue job.

XVII.

Chase Bank's headquarters had replaced, totally, Chemical Bank's old headquartered on Park Avenue. They had torn down the latter and built a new one, nearly entirely subsidized, the white elephant of the arrogant white whale Jaime Dimon, successor to Sandy Weill for whom Dimon had worked at Commercial Credit back in Baltimore. It was something Kurt knew something about, but still he kept his money, what there was of it, in Chase. Now he was on a paper chase.

He got no satisfaction at Chase on Park Avenue - no friend at Chase Manhattan as the old murals falsely promised - so he headed six blocks south to MetroNorth in Grand Central and took the next Harlem Line train up to Tremont Avenue. The little door in the roll down gate at Bande's Luxury Vehicles was open and he went straight in. He had remembered giving the guy here his business card.

"How the hell did you--" Kurt began, then stopped. The man was not alone.

"Him do it," the man said, pointed at Kurt. "Him order the car. Look, he give me this business card to place the order."

As the trio surrounding the man turned and walked toward him, Kurt picked up on that they were law enforcement.

"I came and gave him my card because I am a journalist," Kurt stammered. "The boss of this place is locked up --"

"He's dead," the man said. "It's like I told you. This guy, he got something to do with it."

"It ain't me," Kurt said, or maybe that was just him singing in his head.

"We're gonna take you to the 48th Precinct for a few questions," one of the officers said. "If you tell us everything you know and it checks out, you'll probably be free to leave after that."

Kurt was waiting for the Miranda warning, but it never came. So he didn't call Michael Randall Long. Maybe he could talk his way out of this one. It ain't me, he repeated again and again in his head.

* * * *

The 48th Precinct has green glazed blocks as walls, like precincts and schools of a certain era in New York. He was in a windowless room and they had an old-school video camera set up on a tripod. Another officer was recording with a cell phone.

"Tell me again why you went to the Luxury Car place," the officer said. "Slowly."

"I'm a journalist," Kurt began.

"For who?"

Whom, Kurt thought. "Myself," he answered. The cop laughed. "No," Kurt said, "I mean for my own blog. I started it. A lot of people read it. It is in Google News --"

"Yeah, yeah," the cop said. "So you can to play reporter. What about?"

"A case down in the SDNY," Kurt said. He used the acronym because these guys, if anyone, should know it. They did not appear impressed. "This guy Bande, he was arrested for exactly this: identity theft." Kurt paused. "And now they stole my identity."

"That remains to be seen," the cop said. "And like his partner said, this Bande's been killed in the MDC in Brooklyn." The cop stopped and stared at him, in a way meant to be significant.

Kurt should have asked, Am I a suspect? But he kept thinking he could talk his way out of it.

So Kurt's answers got shorter. As he spoke, such as it was, one of the cops was scrolling through his phone. Speed reading or at least glancing at Kurt's blog, it turned out.

"Tell us again why you went to the body shop?" the cop said, hardly looking up from the phone. "The first time, I mean?"

Kurt repeated, that he'd gone there as a journalist pursuing a story. This time he add, "Under the First Amendment."

The cop looked up from his phone. He laughed. "You call this journalism?" he asked.

"Yeah," Kurt replied. This was one thing he took seriously, since it had gotten him thrown out of the UN. "Yeah I call it journalism, protected by the First Amendment." He paused. "And now," he said, "I'm ending this under the Fifth Amendment."

At least this time the laugh was muffled, or into the hand. "You have a lawyer?" the cop asked.

"I do," Kurt said. "Michael Randall Long." He didn't have Long's business card, but it did remember his address on Worth Street. It wasn't any of there business that this business-sounding address was, in fact, over a fruit stand. "Michael Long of Worth Street."

The cop nodded and they walked out, leaving him in his chair. He couldn't tell if the locked the door behind them, and he wasn't sure if that made a legal difference. He was about to check when the cops returned. One handed him his phone.

"You're free to go," the cop said.

"You've already been free to go," the other added.

"But don't leave town," said the third.

Kurt got up and left without a word.

XVIII.

The 48th Precinct is under the Cross Bronx Expressway. The cars whizzed by above him, still not covered up despite the trillions in the Infrastructure bill. Kurt should have gone up Webster Avenue and then over to the MetroNorth station, or even up Tremont Avenue's hill to the D train on the Grand Concourse.

But instead he walked a block south to 173rd Street, to cross over to the other side of Park Avenue. There were some squatter or homesteading building that he knew there, still looking different from the other, now spruced up houses on the short block. Kurt thought of stopping in but thought, the cops might still be following him. That did not stop him from going past Bande's World of Luxury Cars, and peering in again through the cut-in door.

It didn't talk long.

"There he is, the mother fucker!" Bande's partner yelled. Again he was not alone but the guys with him didn't seem like cops. They ran toward the door, and Kurt ran back out, and south again on Park Avenue. This time he would have to go into the homesteading buildings.

He had nowhere else to seek shelter or protection. Frank's Sporting Goods on the corner of Tremont by the MetroNorth station said it sold hunting rifles but even for that, even open carry, you had to show ID and go through some sort of check, even more so now after the acquittal of Kyle Rittenhouse. So Kurt ran to the homesteaders' house.

"Those ain't nothing but squatters," Kurt heard them yell behind them as he went in. And it was true the front door was side open. Plenio had died some years ago, then Guiermina too. But Kurt still knew the gypsy cab driver on the second floor, now fighting Uber like he had in the past the TLC.

"*Tengo que quedarme un rato con tigo*," Kurt told him at his apartment door.

"'*Ta bien, pana*," the driver said, letting him in and locking the door behind. Inside the apartment was still raw but big speakers blared merengue. The guy took out a large rum bottle that had unidentifiable herbs or seaweed floating in it. "*Vamos a beber*," the driver said. Let's drink. And they did.

XIX.

Michael Randall Long asked to postpone the next Zoom meeting between defense counsel in the Nigerian car ID theft case, as they'd taken to calling it, but the others had all said to go forward. So at the appointed time he walked the block from the courthouse to his office over the fruit stand, fired up the fake background and signed in.

"Terrible what happened to your client," Federal Defender William Kandinsky began, and there was nodding by the other non-Hollywood Squares. "I can share without you some of our sealed pleading to Judge Rakoff, when the ex DEA agent Scheinin died in the MDC."

"Thanks," Long said, thinking how arrogant it was that the Federal Defenders assumed that all CJA lawyers were just lusting to recycle their briefs, especially from a case in which, as he understood it, nothing had been accomplished. "I'm hoping to asked Vratil for a briefing schedule on the death issue."

"You mean, filing in our case?" Kandinsky asked.

"Sure. Isn't that how you all did it in Scheinin?" That, Long had checked on PACER. Judge Rakoff's inquiries, until he ruled nothing out of the ordinary had been found, were all in the docket of the original child pornography case.

"That was a one-defendant case," Kandinsky said. "Here, I don't think the other defendants are going to want to delay accepting the plea offer until your matter plays out." He paused. "How ever it plays out."

"Maybe you all could get a better deal," Long said.

Kandinsky shook his head. "Kudlow said they're not extending the deadline. She says her Office thinks your client's death is just a random shanking."

"Is that the phrase she used?" Long asked.

"I'd have to check my notes," Kandinsky replied.

You do that, Long thought. If he had to file a separate case, he would. Or intervene in this one.

Kurt Wheelock was more than a little drunk when he looked back out the window of the driver's apartment onto 73rd Street. The guys who had chased him in were still there, now around a fire in an oil barrel.

"*Voy a tener que irme*," Kurt said, then asked if there was some other way out, other than through the front door or the fire escape they had welded together on the front.

The driver took him to the basement and, over a pile of rumble, up to a window blocked off with diamond plate. He unlocked it and Kurt saw the lumber yard of Tulnoy's.

"*Puedes salir hasta el tren*," the driver told him: you can go out all the way to the train.

"*El tren* D?"

"*No, el* MetroNorth," the driver said.

At least he'd be able to walk down the tracks a little bit and come out, either up on Tremont or better yet down at the Claremont Parkway station that MetroNorth had closed. He thanked the driver and headed out past the piles of plywood and roofing joists. The old railroad siding was there and Kurt waited. After a time he heard some yelling from out over the yard, voices he may or may not have recognized.

When the train came back it was still only inching along, from the Tremont station. Kurt grabbed a hold of the railing and jumped up on the step. He squeezed in - his backpack was the hardest part - and got between the cars. The yelling had stopped and the sky had turned orange behind him. The squat was on fire. Perhaps it had been lit ablaze. The train was picking up speed.

XXI.

The Religious Freedom press conference at the U.S. State Department was usually pretty straight forward. Under the last president it had gotten a bit more heated, with invective directed at sides in the Middle East that the U.S. usually tried to warily work with. But other than a few hand-wringing op-eds from liberal groups, that too had passed, usually in less than news cycle.

So it was that State Department spokesman approached today's topper, at which he'd read out the list of shame they had distributed half an hour before under embargo to those lounging in the press bullpen, then Blinken would come and read more, take two or three questions. Who could be against religious freedom?

But it wasn't any new addition - there weren't any - but an omission that gave rise to a shouted question before Blinken could even start. It was a guy Hill had once seen once or twice, having called on him the first time and when confronted by a loaded question about Biafra, not called on again.

Prince Nestor from BAN - Biafra and Ambazonia News, he called his outfit, which Hill remembers suggesting in an email that would never be released or even disclosed under

FOIA be look into under FARA, the Foreign Agent Registration Act, or even as a terrorist group - was the one would stood up and yelled.

In the State Department's staid press corpse it was a major breach of protocol. Usually the wire services and long time insiders who took the front two rows, three under COVID, as if it were their birth right asked the first questions, and continue until they were done. Intern from Japanese media and others like Prince Nestor of BAN would wait to see if there were any scraps. Often there weren't.

So Prince Nestor short circuited the closed loop. "Why did Biden drop Nigeria from the list, even as they slaughter our Christian brothers?" he yelled. Hill winced, looking at the robo-cameras on the ceiling, now pointed at Prince Nestor.

Hill cut in: "Mister Nestor -"

"Call me Prince --"

"The Secretary will take one or two questions, some of which are in line in front of you."

"In line? You mean you pre-picked them?" If Sleepy Joe could do it, why not his Blinken?

"It means there are people who have put in some time here," Hill said.

"Like in a jail," Prince Nestor said. "Are you going to answer my Nigeria question?"

It was Blinken who spoke: "Ned will get back to you. I'm sorry, but I've got another meeting upstairs." And Blinken was done, and it was those in the front rows whispering on how to get rid of the little media Prince, who had cost them their canned questions.

XXII.

Kurt had been watching the State Department briefing, as he often did from the 40 Foley Square press room after he'd seen his written questions to the UN he was banned from go unanswered. He'd emailed a few times with Prince Nestor, first when he was still allowed in the UN and could offer advice on how to apply for accreditation, and then after he was thrown out and of lesser use. He liked the guy. So he found the old email chain and wrote to him: Well done! What's up with that? I'm writing a story if you want to send anything.

The response was a press release from a group in Nigeria which had tried to sue Blinken in the DC Federal Court, without success though Judge Amy Berman Jackson had to yet to entirely dismiss the case. They showed a graph of every increased killing of Christians under what they called the Buhari regime. But, Kurt noticed, they didn't mention the United Nations, much less Amina J. Mohammed. Too irrelevant, it seemed. But that's where he came in.

Prince Nestor added, under the press release, "There's a demonstration this afternoon in front of the Nigerian

Mission to the UN. You should go check it out and live stream. I can't get there from DC in time. But I'll link to your live stream. I know your banned from the UN but they can't stop you from going a block away, can they?"

"No they can't," Kurt replied, adding stupidly a smiley face emoji. He charged his phone in anticipation of the live stream.

XXIII.

The glass building on 44th Street and Second Avenue with the Nigerian food truck in front, they called Casa Gambari from the military government's former Ambassador to the UN Ibrahim Gambari, who had been serving dictatorship all the way back to Shell Ogoni killer and thief Sana Abacha.

Now the thievery they delved in was more sophisticated, hacking and identity theft. Today the threat was more physical. The NYPD had set up metal barricades to hold back a crowd of about a hundred people, Kurt figured, shouting about genocide and Buhari. Kurt went through the crowd asking people, with his phone in their face, "What about Amina J. Mohammed?"

"Fulani killer," was one answer.

"Where is she? We ain't see her," was another.

Across the street was a counter-protest, people in white t-shirts that read, Nigeria Must Be One. There was a preprinted sign, "Christians Are Not Being Killed In Nigeria." Kurt thought, Thou dost protest too much.

"Those guys aren't even from Nigeria," one Kurt's interviewees told him. "They got them from the homeless shelter, five dollars a head, to come hold the signs. They figured no one would talk to them so they would just have to look that part."

So Kurt cross Second Avenue to do some interviews.

"What part of Nigeria do you come from?" he asked one protester, drawing a blank stare.

A guy next to him laughed. "Nostrand Avenue," he said.

Kurt had what he needed. And down in DC, so did Prince Nestor of BAN.

XXIV.

"There has to be something we can do," Kurt told Michael Randall Long, pacing around his office, looking out over Worth Street at the SDNY courthouse.

An expedited change of plea proceeding was to begin this morning, all of Bande's co-defendants, or co-defendants before he was killed in the Metropolitan Detention Center. And in a suddenly switch like Judge Nathan was pulling in the Ghislaine Maxwell trial, there would be no call-in line. Long and Kurt would have to go and watch, with Long not able to speak because his client was dead.

"I can't see it, I'm not sure," Long said, which was rare for him. "But I do think we should go."

Unlike the throng from Maxwell, the identity theft change of plea was so low profile there was no problem getting into the courtroom, even into to the first row of the gallery. Judge Vratil looked surprised - was it just at seeing them together? - and William Kamdinsky more so.

"I told you," he took down his mask and mouthed at Long.   Long shrugged.

"I have before me a series of largely identical plea agreements," Judge Vratil said. "They provide for an agreed guideline sentence of a year and a day, with no supervised release to follow." She looked up. "This seems strange," she said to AUSA Kudlow.

"There are factors beyond the four corners of the document," Kudlow said. "I'd be happy to discuss them without your Honor in a closed session."

"I don't do that at sentencing," Judge Vratil said. "Is there a 5K1 letter?" That was the cooperator's Holy Grail.

"Not exactly," Kudlow said. "I mean no, your Honor. And as we told your clerk, we'd like the sentencing done today, like in a Violation of Supervised Release."

"So, without any Pre-Sentencing Report?" Judge Vratil asked. "Are there things your clients would like me to know about them before imposing sentence?"

"We'd waive that in this instance," Kandisky said.

Long stood up. "May I be heard?" he asked Judge Vratil.

"This is most irregular, Mr. Long," Judge Vratil said. "We've already said, you're not in this case."

"I have a victim impact statement," Long said. "I have a victim right here." He pointed down at Kurt Wheelock, who was still sitting.

"Is this covered by the Victim's Rights Act?" Judge Vratil asked AUSA Kudlow. "If it is, I'll have to allow it."

"We don't think so in the first instance," Kudlow sputtered, using the royal we and throwing in the mumbo jumbo about the first instance. "We'd brief it for your Honor but there is no time."

"How is he a victim?" Judge Vratil asked Long. "Did he miss another story or something?"

Kandinstky looked up from scrolling through his phone and laughed.

"No," Long said. "His identity was stolen, by these defendants."

Judge Vratil nodded. "Miss Kudlow?" she asked. "Anything?"

"Not yet," Kudlow answered. "I just heard from my office and we look like to letter-brief this, to avoid this sideshow of a victim's impact statement."

"Like in Epstein's Florida non-prosecution agreement," Kurt whispered loudly to Long, drawing a series of glares from the front.

Kudlow said, "We'll do it before three o'clock and then be prepared to go forward with the allocution and sentencing."

"Miss Bixby?" Judge Vratil asked. "Is that possible?"

"It is, your Honor."

"Three o'clock, then," Judge Vratil. "And beyond putting your letter brief be sure to email a copy to Mr. Long, so he can reply," she said.

"On behalf of my client, I thank you, Judge," Long said, gesturing at Kurt. But he has already stood up and headed to the door.

XXV.

A Citibike would take too long. Kurt took the express 4 train to Grand Central, and then a bike east to First Avenue and the UN. He knew that Amina J. Mohammed liked to drive out with her limousine and two four-by-fours of security to have expensive lunches, like her boss Guterres, and this would be his chance. He fired up his phone to be ready to record.

Two UN Security guards at the gate saw him, and ostentatiously went into their glass booth and picked up the landline phone. It was in there that they had the photo array on which Kurt was shown among the crazies, the guys who'd tried to scale the fence or attack some hapless bureaucrat on the sidewalk. Which Kurt was not above, but Amina J. Mohammed would be in a car.

And here she was now. Kurt turned on the video on his phone and yelled, "I know you did it for Buhari, and to defraud the IMF. It's the one crime you could be held responsible for, swindling an international organization other than the UN." The limousine stopped and the window rolled down.

"Don't you get tired of all this, Mister Wheelock?" Amina J. Mohammed said. "Don't you have anything better to do?"

"I'm intervening in the case down in Federal court. The one in which you had Bande killed," Kurt said.

By now Amina J. Mohammed's drive had rolled down his window and asked his passenger, "Do you want me to call our friends in the NYPD?"

"No," Amina J. Mohammed replied. "Let him in this time. I feel an obligation to hear out these allegations."

An obligation to your real boss Buhari, Kurt thought, not the equally corrupt Guterres. But he got in.

* * * *

The car drove downtown and through the tunnel to New Jersey. "I looked into it, after the first allegation by your lawyer Mr. Long. He is your lawyer, right?"

"Yes," Kurt said. "And his next case is going to be to sue you and Melissa Fleming for keeping me banned from the UN, not even acting on my applications for accreditation."

"Sound like a winner," Amina J. Mohammed said, with a smirk. "Anyway I looked into the car business, even the car you claim you're the victim in."

"They used my name," Kurt said. "You used my name."

"You'll see that's not the case. We're going there now."

The car turned into a compound with shipping container stacked high, a steel wound of Sleepy Joe's supply chain disease.

"Trump played around the China and this is what they got," Amina J. Mohammed said. "But these cars were pre-booked, including yours."

The container stood conveniently alone under a big claw of a crane. "My driver will show you, the sticker that on the windscreen."

Wind SHIELD, Kurt thought. But he followed the driver into the container, his phone still recording, if only audio since it was in his pocket.

"You can only see it from inside the car, inside the glove box," the driver said.

Glove COMPARTMENT, Kurt thought. He leaned in and opened it then felt like a bolt of lightening on the top of his head.

When he came too it was entirely dark and the container was rocking, every so slightly. He tried to turn on his phone but it had run out of battery.

The story, it seemed, would be untold or not concluded.

End of Part I

www.ingramcontent.com/pod-product-compliance
Lightning Source LLC
Chambersburg PA
CBHW071450150726
48000CB00006B/2508